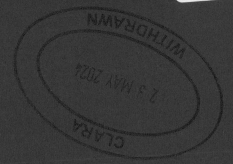

# GULLIVER

## JONATHAN SWIFT

### RETOLD BY MARY WEBB

illustrated by

LAUREN O'NEILL

THE O'BRIEN PRESS
DUBLIN

First published 2015 by
The O'Brien Press Ltd,
12 Terenure Road East, Rathgar,
Dublin 6, D06 HD27, Ireland.
Tel: +353 1 4923333; Fax: +353 1 4922777
E-mail: books@obrien.ie
Website: www.obrien.ie
ISBN: 978-1-84717-676-9

8 7 6 5 4 3 2 1
18 17 16 15

Printed and bound in Poland by Białostockie Zakłady Graficzne S.A.
The paper in this book is produced using pulp from managed forests.

# CONTENTS

This book is based on *Gulliver's Travels* by Jonathan Swift (1667–1745). Published in 1726, *Gulliver's Travels* is a satire, a type of writing that pokes fun at people and institutions — especially if they are powerful, pompous or cruel. Swift enjoyed ridiculing anyone who took themselves too seriously, including politicians, scientists, churchmen, and royalty.

Part I of Swift's book, 'A Voyage to Lilliput', is one of literature's most famous stories. Through Gulliver's eyes, Swift shows us how petty and silly the little people of Lilliput are, especially in their ambitions for power. In Part II, 'A Voyage to Brobdingnag', he shows us the opposite point of view, that when one is small and powerless, life is full of danger.

Swift teaches us that, whether our position in life is as lofty as a giant's or as insignificant as a fly's, we are all human beings, and worthy of respect.

# PART I
# GULLIVER IN THE LAND OF LILLIPUT

My name is Gulliver, and I have a tale to tell that will make your hair stand up and your mouth hang open.

All I ever wanted was to travel and have amazing adventures. So one spring day, I threw some clothes into a bag, said goodbye to my shocked family, and boarded the *Antelope,* a ship bound for the Tropics.

We sailed east into the rising sun. My work was not hard. There was plenty to eat, and the other lads were lively. When we stopped for food or water, there were exciting places to visit. I was having a wonderful time.

But one night, all this changed …

'Bad weather coming,' said the Captain grimly. In no time, the sea was black, the waves were huge, and the mast was creaking fit to snap off.

The gale hit us like a massive hammer. The crew worked hard, but by the time the wind died down, we were lost. Much as I loved adventure, *this* was not what I'd had in mind.

But worse was yet to come.

A dense, ghostly fog floated down, and we couldn't see where we were going. Suddenly, looming out of nowhere, was a massive rock! We tried to steer away but it was too late. We smashed straight into it, the ship split in two, and we were all thrown into the freezing sea.

I swam for the rock as hard as I could. But the fog was like an icy white curtain, and I could see nothing.

'Help!' I shouted, but there was no answer. I was all alone.

I swam and swam until my arms and legs felt like burning lumps of lead. Just as I was about to give up and drown, my foot touched something solid beneath me. It was sand – I was saved!

I staggered out of the sea and fell over on some grass. I was so tired, I could not get up again, and I slipped into a deep, deep sleep.

When I woke up, it was daylight and I was very thirsty. I blinked up at the clear, sunny sky and tried to move.

But I couldn't. I tried again, but I couldn't move at all – not even to turn my head! I peered out of the corner of my eye. There were thin ropes all over my body, tying me firmly to the ground. Even my hair was tied down!

What on earth was happening?

6

Hours passed. The sun beat down on me and all I could think of was water.

Then I felt a tickle on my leg. A spider, perhaps? Or a scorpion? I wanted to scratch it, but couldn't reach. The tickle travelled up my body and onto my chest.

I wriggled and peered down – and I got the biggest shock of my whole life.

Standing on my chest, with his arms crossed, was a teeny, tiny little man! A human being, perfect in every way, except that he was no bigger than my finger.

Behind him stood about fifty other little men, just the same size – and they all carried wicked little bows and arrows.

Was I dead? Was I dreaming? I blinked hard. The little men were real.

'Who are you?' I shouted. '*What* are you?'

The creatures ran off in all directions, yelping and covering their ears. I pulled free one arm and my hair from the ropes. I raised my head – and soon wished I hadn't.

Hundreds of the little men were marching up the beach towards me, like an army. The front row drew back their bows and fired a shower of arrows, straight at my face and arm. The arrows stung like the devil, and I lay down again, fast.

There was no escape. I was at the mercy of the strange little men.

The leader of the little men climbed onto a wooden platform right beside my head. He made a long speech, using hand signs and his own odd language.

But by now I was so hungry and thirsty, I could think of nothing else. 'Food,' I croaked, pointing to my mouth and my stomach.

The leader nodded to some little men, who rushed off up the beach. When they came back, they carried dozens of loaves of bread and barrels of wine. They climbed onto my chest, walked to my mouth and tipped the food in, bit by bit.

I was very tempted to knock them all off my chest with my free hand and try to escape, but they seemed kinder now. They even pulled the tiny arrows out of my hands and face, and rubbed a soothing cream into my cuts.

I let them know I badly needed a wee. They loosened the ropes a little. I turned on my side, where I made so much water that it was like a gushing river. They all had to jump clear, before they were washed away!

Soon, I began to yawn and found I couldn't keep my eyes open. Then I realized why they were no longer afraid of me. They had put a sleeping potion in my wine!

When I woke again, I was still tied up — but moving along on a wooden raft, which was pulled by hundreds of little horses, the same size as mice. The little people must have built it while I was asleep.

Over the next few days, I was kept on the raft. I talked to the leader and picked up enough of the language to understand that I was in a place called Lilliput, the greatest nation in the world. We were going to the capital city, where the mighty Emperor lived. He wanted to see me, and would decide whether I was to live or die.

'Don't get your hopes up,' the little man said. 'We can't afford to feed a Man-Mountain like you!'

I was guarded all the time by hundreds of armed men. One morning, two or three of them climbed onto my chest to get a better look at me. One of them crept to my chin and poked a tiny pike right up my nose. Of course, I sneezed and sent them all flying off my chest. Luckily, only their pride was hurt.

After two days, we reached the city. It was just like a doll's town with red, green, blue and yellow buildings and streets set out neatly in a square. We stopped, and the leader showed off a long, low stone building.

'Behold! The biggest building in Lilliput!' he said proudly. 'This is where you will stay.'

I peered at my new home, and tried not to worry that it only came up to my knees.

The Emperor's blacksmiths arrived carrying two or three little chains. I laughed. They were thinner than my watch chain and would never hold me! However, my laughter died out when more and more chains arrived.

In all, the blacksmiths wrapped ninety-one chains around my leg with thirty-six padlocks, and fastened the other ends to the wall of my new house.

When they were sure that I couldn't run off, they cut all my other ropes. I got up slowly onto my hands and knees. I crept into my house through a doorway in one end. Inside, I lay down — the building was the same length as me so there was just enough room. Falling asleep, I wondered what on earth would happen next.

The next morning, an excited crowd of little people buzzed around outside my house, wanting to see the Man-Mountain. I crawled out, and I stood up for the first time in three days, stretching to my full length. The crowd gawped at me, and fell back in wonder.

As I gazed over the town and the beautiful countryside around it, I spotted a splendid procession coming towards me on horseback. The Emperor of Lilliput and his Court had come to view the giant that had washed up on his island.

The Emperor was a fine specimen of manhood, being about a fingernail taller than his subjects. On his noble head, he wore a golden helmet studded with jewels that sparkled in the sunlight, and he carried a magnificent golden sword.

Behind him, at a safe distance, sat the dignified little Empress, with the young princes and princesses. They were so finely dressed that, all together, they looked like a fancy petticoat spread out on the ground with laces and ruffles and sequins and gold and silver thread. They all smiled at me.

The imperial horse wasn't happy though. He reared and snorted and backed away. The Emperor nearly fell off, so he got down and walked right up to me.

'Your Majesty,' I said and bowed low.

He snapped his fingers, and thirty men came forward pushing wheelbarrows full of meat and wine. I tipped each barrow down my throat until there was not a crumb or a drop left, and then I lay down in front of the Emperor so my face could be level with him.

The Emperor then made a long, *long* speech welcoming me to Lilliput. The crowd clapped and cheered loudly. I sat up and hid my yawns by bowing my head many times.

After the imperial family returned to the palace, the little people pressed closer and closer to me, getting cheekier and cheekier.

I began to be a little afraid of them.

Suddenly, arrows came flying out of nowhere – some of the little people were shooting at me! I tried to scramble into my house, but an arrow hit me in the face, and nearly took out my eye!

'Hey! Who did that?' the captain of the guard shouted. He rounded up six of the little archers, tied their hands behind their backs, and brought them to me. They stared up at me, quaking in their tiny boots.

At last, I thought, a chance to have a bit of fun! I scooped them all up in one hand, and dropped five into my pocket. I held up the sixth little man to my open mouth, as though I intended to eat him, like an ogre in a fairytale.

'Yum, yum,' I said and patted my tummy.

The poor creature nearly passed out and a great gasp came up from the crowd. When I took out my penknife, they all screamed.

But I had no intention of harming any living creature, no matter how small. I cut the strings that tied the little man's hands, then I set him gently down on the ground. I took the other five out of my pocket and did the same with them.

Great cheers rang out from the crowd. Soon after, night fell on Lilliput and people began to go home, waving and blowing little kisses to me. I waved back, being careful not to wallop anyone by accident.

I heard later that the Emperor was delighted with my merciful behaviour towards his people.

Food and drink arrived by wheelbarrow every day. I had plenty of water to wash in. When I had to go to the toilet, I went in the field behind my house, and some men with clothes pegs on their noses would come and cart everything away.

But, at night, I slept badly on the cold, stone floor. When the Emperor heard this, he ordered workmen to get busy and create a bed and some covers for me.

So, one morning, I awoke to find huge piles of sheets and hundreds of mattresses outside my house, gathered from all over the kingdom! The workmen sewed six hundred mattresses together to make a bed big enough, and then they sewed nine hundred sheets together to make a cover that was long enough. Hundreds of them worked all day until the job was done.

I was thrilled with my cosy new bed. I thanked the tired workers many times. Then I dragged the bed inside, lay down in it and slept like a log.

The news of my arrival spread across the land. Every day crowds of people came, from far and near, to look at the Man-Mountain. No longer afraid, they climbed and ran and danced all over me. When I lay down, their children played hide and seek in my hair. I loved to see them so happy, but I hated being in chains.

The next time the Emperor visited, I fell on my knees before him, causing a small earth tremor.

'I beg you, Your Majesty,' I said. 'Please remove my chains!'

'Hmm, we shall see,' replied the Emperor, frowning.

I was a bit worried. The Emperor's main advisor was the Admiral, and he did not like me. If he had his way, I would never be free …

But on his next visit, the Emperor was all smiles again.

'Gulliver, I believe you are harmless,' he said. 'Even so, my guards will search you, top to toe. It could take a while.'

'I agree,' I said. 'Let it be done as soon as possible.'

'How about now?' said the Emperor and clapped his hands. Instantly (because that's what happens when you're an Emperor), a man appeared carrying a pen and paper, followed by two officers of the guard. I lifted these two up and allowed them a free run of my pockets (all except one, which was a secret pocket with things in it I wanted to keep). This was what they found:

23

My handkerchief, which was listed as 'a great piece of cloth, big enough to carpet the Emperor's ballroom'.

My snuff-box, which was listed as 'a huge silver chest full of strange dust' (One of the foolish guards jumped into it, and the snuff made him sneeze so much he had to go to bed).

My comb, which was listed as 'a great engine with twenty long poles sticking out of the back'.

My knife and razor, which were listed as 'two long plates of steel'.

My purse with my money inside, which was listed as 'round flat pieces of yellow and white metal that the Man-Mountain thinks are valuable'.

My round, silver watch, which was listed as 'a great engine, in the shape of a globe. It makes a terrible noise, like a water-mill, and there are strange figures drawn on it, with an arrow that moves very slowly. We believe that it may be a god that the Man-Mountain worships, for he told us that it rules almost every action of his life.'

My pistols, gunpowder and bullets were added to the list, along with my sword.

Their work done, the guards presented the list to the Emperor, who asked to see my sword. I whipped it out from its scabbard rather quickly, and there were cries of alarm from the guards. It was, after all, the length of five little men. The brave Emperor himself did not show any fear.

Next, he asked to see how one of my pistols worked. I filled the pistol with gunpowder, pushed in a bullet, and fired it into the air.

BANG!

Dozens of the little people fell to the ground as though they had been shot and even the Emperor himself went a bit of a funny colour.

One by one, I gave up all the things that were on the list, including my weapons and my watch. (Luckily the things I kept back in my secret pocket, including my glasses, were not discovered.)

To my great joy, the Emperor agreed to free me from chains, so long as I followed some rules. These were:

*Do not* leave the country without permission.

*Do not* walk in the fields where there are crops, walk only on the main roads.

*Do* give two hours' notice before walking in the city, so that people can stay out of the way.

*Do* help Lilliput against its enemies, especially the wicked kingdom of Blefuscu.

I agreed to follow all the rules, and the blacksmiths came and unlocked my chains. I was free at last!

The first thing to do was explore Lilliput's main city.

'Don't forget to visit us at the Grand Palace,' said the Emperor. So the next day, I set off.

I moved slowly through the city. Most people had gone into their houses, but I could still see them through their tiny windows, working, eating and playing. One or two brave souls climbed up on the rooftops to get closer to me. I had to be very careful not to sweep the pesky little daredevils off with the ends of my coat.

I was astonished at the size and bustle of the city, which held half a million little people. Everywhere there were shops, markets, parks and churches. The colourful houses had gardens that were only the size of a postage stamp. I stepped easily from one main street to the next, but I could not go down the alleys and passages, for they were too narrow for my feet.

The Emperor's palace was in the middle of the city, surrounded by walls. I stepped over the outside walls into the inner courtyard of the palace itself.

I lay down on the ground and peeked through the palace windows. The rooms were splendid, with beautiful fireplaces and gold and silver candleholders. The flames from the candles glittered in the mirrors and made the crystal glasses on the dining table sparkle. It was like a little wonderland.

I heard a tap-tap against an upstairs window. It was the Empress herself in her own rooms. She smiled and held out her hand through the window so that I could kiss it. Behind her, the little princes and princesses giggled and waved.

After this, there was no stopping me. I spent many happy days exploring Lilliput, down as far as the coast and all around the countryside. I often visited the palace, and the Emperor and I became great friends.

One day, the Emperor ordered a cavalry parade in front of the palace. He commanded me to stand with legs astride the courtyard, like an arch, so the riders could go underneath me. Unfortunately, halfway through the parade I saw them laughing and pointing upwards at me as they passed. I fear that my trousers were by now so full of holes, that the cavalry saw more of me than they should have!

Another day, I arrived just as some nervous-looking courtiers were getting ready to do 'rope-dancing'.

'What on earth is that?' I asked, peering at the tightrope stretched across the courtyard.

'It's how I decide who gets a good job at my Court,' said the Emperor.

The courtiers each had to walk the tightrope to the middle. Then they had to jump as high as they could, and try to land back on the rope. If they jumped high enough and amused His Majesty, they got a good job and earned plenty of money. But if they fell off, not only did they look foolish, they also risked breaking a bone. And, of course, they got nothing.

I thought it was the silliest thing I'd seen in Lilliput, but I did not dare say so to the Emperor.

Soon I got a chance to repay the Emperor and Empress for their kindness.

Near Lilliput, there was an island called Blefuscu, which was also full of little people. The two countries had been at war for three years. And do you know what the quarrel was about? The correct way to crack open a boiled egg!

It all started many years before, when the Emperor's grandfather was a boy. One morning, he had a boiled egg for breakfast. Now, as we know, there is a bigger end and a smaller end to an egg, and it doesn't matter which end you crack. But, when the Emperor's grandfather broke open the big end that morning, he cut his finger by accident.

Immediately, a command went out from the palace: No one was ever to crack an egg at the big end again. They were always to use the small end – or be put to death!

Of course, this made some people angry, and they rebelled against the law. They wanted to crack their eggs at the big end, if they felt like it. The rebels became known as the Big-Endians, and they fought many times with the Emperor. You wouldn't believe how many little people lost their lives! Some Big-Endians fled to the island of Blefuscu to plot revenge against Lilliput.

Now, the Emperor of Blefuscu was ready to attack Lilliput with fifty warships, and win the argument, once and for all.

Messengers came to tell me that the Emperor was asking for my help. Was there anything the Man-Mountain could do to stop Blefuscu from invading Lilliput?

I thought hard and came up with a brilliant plan.

'Fetch me a length of the strongest cable you can make and one hundred and fifty iron bars,' I said to the blacksmiths, and they ran to do my bidding.

I plaited together lengths of cable to make an even thicker cable. Then I twisted together three iron bars and bent them into a hook. When I had made many thick cables and hooks, I put a hook at the end of each cable. I hung them all over my shoulders, hoping I had made enough. It certainly felt like it. They weighed a ton.

From the beach, I could see across to the island of Blefuscu. The ships were bobbing in the harbour, ready for war, with their crews on board and their guns loaded.

The Emperor and all the Court gathered on the shore to see me off. I took off my shoes and stockings, and stepped into the water. I walked to the middle of the channel that separated the two islands. I then swam where the water was deeper, which was not easy with half a ton of metal hanging off me. When I was near the Blefuscu side, I stood up again.

When the sailors saw a Man-Mountain looming out of the sea in front of them, they screamed in terror and ran for it. Some of them jumped overboard, to get away from me all the quicker. Soon all the ships were deserted.

But I was not finished yet. I hooked a cable onto the front of each ship, and gathered the ends together. I was going to steal the entire fleet!

Suddenly I felt a sharp stinging all over my arms and body. The brave little men of Blefuscu had come back to defend their ships, and were now firing hundreds of arrows at me. I remembered how an arrow had nearly blinded me before, so I took my glasses from my secret pocket and put them on.

I heaved and tugged on the cables with all my might to get the ships moving — but they were firmly anchored to the seabed. There was nothing for it, I had to cut off all the anchors. When the sailors saw this, they shouted and howled and rained down even more arrows on me.

I pulled again at the cables. This time, all the ships floated after me. When I got to the middle of the channel where it was deep, I had to swim while pulling the ships, and I don't know how I didn't drown. As soon as the water grew shallow, I rose up in triumph.

'Long live the Emperor of Lilliput!' I shouted.

A cheer went up from the crowd. The Emperor was grinning from ear to tiny ear.

I was a huge success. Not only had I saved the country from their enemies, but I had brought them a brand new fleet of warships as well! On the spot, the Emperor gave me a title. From now on, I was to be called Sir Gulliver, Champion of Lilliput.

But it is strange just how fickle rulers can be. The Emperor should have been content with what I had done for him, but he wasn't.

'Man-Mountain,' he said, rubbing his little hands together greedily. 'Now we've seen you in action, let's conquer the whole of Blefuscu together! We'll get rid of those Big-Endians once and for all — and I will be King of the World!'

This made me unhappy. Why would I want to harm people just to make the Emperor more powerful? Why could he not learn to live in peace with his neighbours? Ambassadors from Blefuscu had come to Lilliput with peace offerings of gold and jewels, yet still the Emperor was not satisfied!

So I refused to help him make slaves of people. He became so angry, he would not speak to me. The Admiral told everyone that I was out of favour, so no one else would speak to me either. That night, the ambassadors from Blefuscu visited me in secret.

'Thank you, Man-Mountain, for not enslaving us,' they said. 'We fear your Emperor has gone power-mad.'

I said nothing, out of loyalty.

'Please, please, come to us in Blefuscu!' they said.

'I'll think about it,' I said. To tell the truth, I was beginning to feel scared of what might happen to me in Lilliput.

And then I did something that really got me into trouble.

At midnight I was woken by the smell of smoke and the shouts of people outside. What in heaven's name was happening now? A messenger from the Emperor appeared.

'The palace is on fire!' he gasped. 'Please come quickly!'

I lost no time. I raced to the palace, trying not to flatten any little people who were crowding the streets in panic. At the palace, I found a chain of people passing buckets of water to try and put out the fire, which was in the Empress's rooms. But the buckets were the size of thimbles and the flames were leaping higher and higher by the minute.

I had one of my brilliant ideas. I had drunk a lot at bedtime, and was now dying for a wee. I won't go into details, but let's just say that I unbuttoned my breeches and within three minutes the fire was totally out!

I looked around proudly, expecting cheers and applause for my quick thinking. Instead, a deathly silence fell on the crowd and they all stared at me. I returned to my house quickly. Even though I had saved the palace, I had a feeling the Empress would not be happy with me.

And I was right. Under the laws of Lilliput, it was high treason to make water in — or in this case *all over* — the Grand Palace. The Empress was so horrified at what I had done, she refused to set foot in her rooms ever again. I had committed a terrible crime — and might be required to pay with my life.

Now that both the Emperor and Empress were angry, my enemies at Court could gossip and do me great harm. The Admiral was saying that Lilliput would be better off without me. I cost too much to feed, I could turn traitor at any time, and I had committed a crime.

Ungrateful creature — after everything I had done for Lilliput!

One evening, a friend arrived and told me that the Admiral was making a plan to kill me! My few supporters at Court were begging for mercy for me. One said the Emperor shouldn't kill me, but blind me instead, so that at least I could carry on working!

'Man-Mountain, go to Blefuscu,' said my friend. 'This very night, if you can!'

He was right. The time had come for me to escape from Lilliput, or die in the attempt.

Later that dark night, I crept to the coast and waded into the water. I towed a warship behind me as a gift for the Emperor of Blefuscu. When I arrived, the Emperor welcomed me (and my ship) with a feast. He was so grateful for my former mercy to his people that he lavished presents on me, including gold coins, which were so small I could hardly see them, a portrait of himself, and a herd of teeny, weeny sheep.

One morning, while walking on the shore of Blefuscu, I found a rowboat. It was big, not tiny, so it must have blown in from a passing ship during a storm. It gave me a daring idea. Why shouldn't I sail away in it?

I set to work mending, patching and waterproofing the boat until it was ship-shape. Finally, I was ready to take my chance on the open sea.

The Emperor gave me his blessing, and secretly looked relieved that I was leaving, and taking my massive appetite with me. I set sail and, after some rough weather and a period with no food, I was rescued by a ship bound for Europe. I was going home at last.

It was wonderful to be reunited with my family, who had thought I was lost at sea. At first, no one believed a word of my story, and insisted that I had sunstroke. But they changed their minds when I showed them the tiny sheep. And ever since, I have made a good living out of telling my amazing tale – Gulliver's adventures in Lilliput, the Land of the Little People.

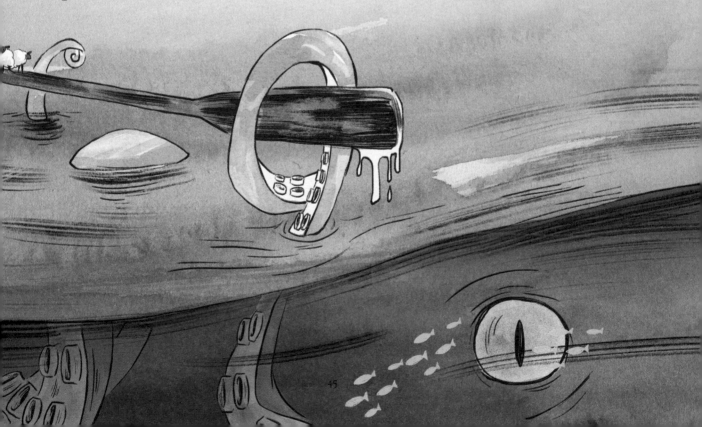

PART II

**GULLIVER IN THE LAND OF THE GIANTS**

Adventure

After nearly losing my life among the little people of Lilliput, you'd think that I would have settled down. But not a chance!

Only two months after coming home, I was restless again, so off I went down to the docks. This time, I found a job on a ship bound for India. It was called the *Adventure*, which turned out to be a very fitting name, as you will see …

At first, all went well. The skies were blue, the breeze was warm, and the sea sparkled.

But just after we left the Cape of Good Hope in Africa, a grey cloud swirled over us and a terrible storm blew up out of nowhere. The ship was thrown from side to side by the wind and waves. The next thing I knew, I was battling alongside the crew to save us from capsizing. This went on all night, but by sunrise the storm had passed and the sea became calm once again. We had survived.

The Captain, however, still looked unhappy.

'The bad news is, we're lost,' he said. 'The worse news is, we've got only two barrels of fresh water on board.'

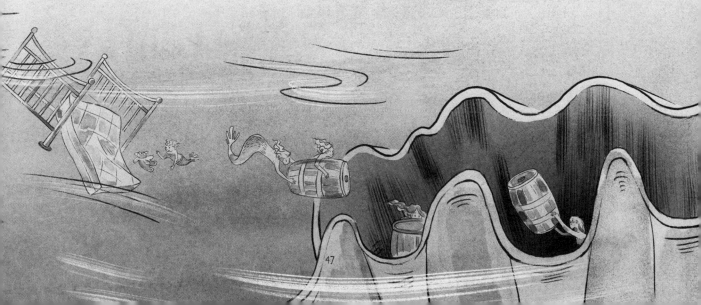

We all knew that we would not survive long without water. We had to find land — and fast.

We sailed south and it grew hotter. After one day, my lips cracked. After two days, I had no spit in my mouth. After three days, I had no tears left. But the next day, I heard a sailor shout the two most wonderful words in the world:

'Land Ho!'

I raced to the front of the ship. Sure enough, there it was: a large, rocky island. The Captain stared at all his maps. Then he stared at them upside down and back to front, but he still could not find this island on any of them.

Twelve crew rowed to the shore in a small rowboat. Their mission was to find water and fill the barrels. I went along too, keen to explore. Perhaps I would find some new shells or plants for my collection — or even some buried treasure. As the crew set off down the beach, I started up a steep hill to get a good view over this strange island.

At the top of the hill, I glanced back towards the beach. To my total horror, I saw my crewmates jumping back into our boat, and rowing away as if their lives depended on it! They were leaving me behind!

But why? As I opened my mouth to yell after them, I saw what they were running away from, and my words froze on my lips …

For there, wading through the water and shaking his fist, was a massive, angry giant!

This hideous sight made me whimper with fear. He was ten times bigger than a man — about twenty metres tall! His legs made gigantic strides through the sea, and he soon began to catch up with my petrified crewmates. But all of a sudden, he roared in pain and lifted his foot out of the water. He had stubbed it on a sharp rock.

My crewmates used the delay to row all the harder. Within minutes, they had disappeared into the distance. The giant growled after them and limped back towards the shore — and me.

I'll admit it, I panicked. I ran around the hilltop like a mad thing. How was I going to get away? Apart from the sea, there was nothing but vast fields full of corn stretching out for miles. I raced down a path through the nearest field. All the crops were five times my height, and I could not see where I was going.

I came to a stone stile, or steps, that led into the next field — but each step was the same height as me and impossible to climb. I was trapped.

Then the earth started to shake, and I heard the sound I had been dreading. Booming voices were coming closer and closer. A huge head, the size of a massive cartwheel, appeared over the top of the stile, followed by a huge body. The giant crashed into the field and shouted behind him in a voice like thunder. My heart nearly stopped.

Seven more giants appeared, each one taller than a church tower and each one carrying a sharp, curved slash-hook.

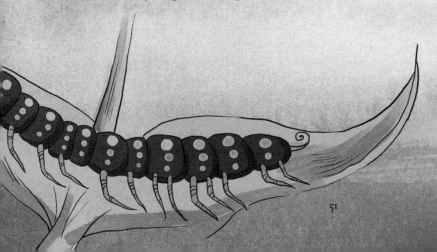

The giants all set to work cutting the crop, slashing great armfuls of corn with every stroke. Terrified, I ran. I kept just ahead of the deadly blades, but I fell over a few times and the giants' feet barely missed crushing my skull. How long could I keep this up?

It was no good. I would be squashed, or sliced, or both. I stopped running and drew a deep breath.

'Hey!' I shouted, waving my arms. 'Down here!'

The nearest giant stopped and squinted down at me. His mouth gaped open in shock. Then he picked me up gently and held me in front of his eyes.

Close up, a giant is an ugly thing, let me tell you. This one's skin was full of black holes, the hairs in his nose were as coarse as a pig's bristles, and his breath nearly knocked me out.

The giant dangled me across the field to his master, the farmer, and handed me over. The farmer's eyes grew big as saucers at the sight of me, a tiny man, sitting in the palm of his hand. He measured me against his middle finger — I was exactly the same size as it. Soon all the workers were gathered around me, oohing and aahing.

The farmer put me down. As soon as I was safe on solid ground, I dropped onto my knees.

'Mercy, master!' I cried, clasping my hands. 'I am a person just like you!'

The giants just stared at me, so I got up. Perhaps if I showed them a few tricks, maybe — just maybe — they wouldn't stamp out my life, as if I were a beetle. So I stood on my hands and turned a few somersaults. They howled with ear-splitting laughter, and my new master rubbed his chin and looked thoughtful. He sent the others back to work, picked me up, and carried me home.

My master's wife came to the door to meet him. When she saw me sitting in his hand, she shrieked and shrank back, as if I were a toad or other loathsome creature. But my master poked me to show her I was harmless and, after a while, she held out her own hand for me.

Good manners are very important, wherever you find yourself, so I took my hat off and bowed as low as I could. The wife was pleased at this, and carried me inside to show her children. There they sat, goggle-eyed, as I was set down on the table. I took care to keep as far away from the edge as possible.

It was dinnertime, and the giant's children were hungry. Luckily I wasn't on the menu. In fact, I was pretty hungry myself. While they slurped stew from bowls as big as swimming pools, and munched potatoes the size of giant footballs, I took my own knife and fork from my pocket. My master's wife mashed some food for me. Then they all looked on, delighted, as I ate.

After dinner, a nurse came in carrying an enormous baby. All of a sudden, the child reached over and grabbed me, as if I were a rattle. He squeezed me fit to break my ribs, and then he put my head in his mouth and covered me with baby slobber. The nurse scolded him, and breastfed him to keep him quiet. Her breast was the same size as me and the nipple that went into his mouth was almost the size of my head!

The wife dried me off then laid me gently on her own pillow in the room next door, with a clean handkerchief to cover me. I fell asleep straight away, and dreamed of home.

But there was to be no rest for me. A nudge on my foot woke me. To my horror, not one but *two* brown rats the size of wolves were crawling up the bed towards me, sniffing.

'Help! Help me!' I screamed, but no one in the other room could hear my voice. It was up to me to defend myself.

My hand gripped my sword handle. The first rat bared his fangs and got ready to attack. I leapt up. The rat went for my throat but, as he did so, I plunged my sword straight through his heart. He keeled over, covered in blood and stone dead.

'Who's next?' I growled at the second rat. He took one look at his friend, and scampered away.

I collapsed, blubbing, on the bed. How on earth was I going to survive here, where even the rodents were monsters?

My master's wife soon found me.

'What a mess!' she boomed. 'Glum! Glummy!'

Her youngest daughter, Glumdalclitch, a gentle little girl of about ten metres tall, trotted in, lifted me and rocked me in her arms.

The first thing Glum did was make a safe place for me to sleep. She filled her doll's cradle with soft sheep's wool, covered with a cloth. Then she placed the cradle on a shelf near her bed, where no rats or mice could get at it.

Next, she made me a new set of clothes, since mine were in tatters. The stitches were very big and the fabric was scratchy, but I was so grateful that I could not complain.

Glum called me her little Mannikin, and carried me everywhere. She told me I was in the land of Brobdingnag, and taught me her strange language. I still had to shout at the top of my voice, which was no more than a squeak to these giants. Yet they thought *they* were the normal ones, and *I* was the oddity! Gazing up at them, I could at last understand how I had looked to the little people of Lilliput.

Every day, more people came to the farmhouse to stare at me. This gave my master an idea.

'Pack him up, Glum, we are going to market,' he said. 'People will pay good money to see an oddity like him.'

Soft-hearted Glum cried when she heard this. She was afraid that rough people would squeeze me and break all my bones. I was a bit nervous about that myself, but I did want to go. Secretly, I was hoping that, on the journey, I might find some way to escape and get back to my own country.

The next morning my master put me in a box, and hung it off his horse. Glum climbed up behind him and off we went. I spent the whole journey being thrown about like a rag doll. But that, believe me, was just the beginning of my troubles.

When we reached town, my master set my box on a vast table in an old inn.

'Ladies and gentlemen,' said Glum. 'I give you the one, the only, Marvellous Mannikin!'

The giants crowded round me and I played my part. I marched across the table, bowing and saying 'Welcome! Welcome!' in their own language. I drew my sword and cut lengths of straw into tiny pieces. I drank out of a nutshell. Every time I did anything, they clapped and cheered, almost deafening me.

Again and again the room filled up. No sooner had one crowd left than another took their place. I grew very tired but my master would not let me stop. The pile of coins in his money box was growing higher and higher, but still he was not satisfied.

In the tenth crowd, a nasty boy threw a hazelnut at my head. To me, it was the size of a pumpkin and, if I had not managed to duck, it would have killed me. Only then did my master call a halt to my work.

I fell into my box. I was shattered, and I slept all the way home.

My master was so delighted with the money I had made for him that he began to think big.

'I bet the King and Queen will pay good money to see this,' he said. 'Glum, prepare him for a visit to the palace!'

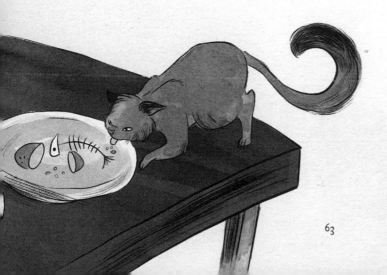

Once again, Glum packed our bag and we set off on a long, weary journey to the big city where the palace was. My master stopped at every town and village on the way, and I entertained crowds of giants, day after day. At night, I crawled into my box, too tired even to eat.

And I saw some sights, I can tell you. The deep scars on faces, the thick stumps of beards, the giant who banged around on two wooden legs, each ten metres high. The worse thing was the lice; they were enormous, and I could see their arms and legs as they crawled on the giants' clothes and in their hair …

I grew thin and pale. Glum begged her father to let me rest. But when my master saw the money pouring in, his eyes grew mad with greed, and he worked me harder still.

The day we reached the city, a message from the palace was waiting. The Queen commanded us to come straight away.

'Now our fortunes are made!' my master said, rubbing his hands in glee.

'Our fortunes?' I squeaked. *'I'm* doing all the work, not you!'

But I was too little and powerless to be heard. Instead my master just packed me into my box and slammed the lid.

The palace was so large that I could not see from one end of it to the other. Made completely of white marble, its roof was two hundred metres high and its walls thirty metres thick. The Queen and her ladies were waiting for us. They were gloriously dressed; although, being a warm day, they did pong a bit. But then, most giants do.

Glum opened my box. Out I stepped and bowed low.

'Greetings from Europe!' I cried. 'I thank Your Majesty for receiving me!'

The Queen smiled and held out her hand. I kissed the tip of her little finger.

'You have come far, lovely little Mannikin!' she said. 'Do tell me of your own country.'

So I talked for a few minutes, and Her Majesty was enchanted. At last, she offered my master a thousand pieces of gold for me, and he accepted on the spot. He thought I would die soon anyway, and he was keen to have me off his hands.

I was happy to part company with him too, but I told the Queen that I could not leave my little nurse, Glum. Her Majesty agreed the girl could stay and look after me. And so my master got a double good deal — a pile of gold *and* a good job for his daughter at the palace. He snatched his money, left us without even saying goodbye, and rushed home, gloating.

Next, I was tidied up and prepared to met the King. I was nervous, for I was told that he was as stern as the Queen was friendly.

At first, he insisted I was a piece of clockwork and not human at all. He had me examined under a magnifying glass by his doctors, and fired many questions at me. From my answers, he finally decided I was not a machine sent to him as a joke, but a sensible little animal.

I told him all about my travels, but when I described Lilliput, he laughed long and hard. A land where the people were even smaller than I was? A land where I was a giant? Impossible! I was sent away to my supper, and then off to bed.

He had many talks with me after that. He was surprised to hear about my country, especially that people as small as me should think themselves important enough to have a government and an army. He also couldn't understand why the silly little people of my country invaded other people's countries and took them over. He had a point.

'Insects!' he bellowed. 'They are nothing but strutting, prattling insects!'

The Queen was much kinder. She gave me a gold ring off her little finger, which I wore as a collar. She ordered a special room to be made for me to sleep in, and it was the most beautiful thing I have ever seen. It was a large, airy box that was quilted on all sides with cotton, and it had windows, and a door with a lock. There were chairs, a table, a wardrobe and a proper bed, all made by a master carpenter.

She had a pair of soft breeches made for me out of a mouse's skin, and ordered a silver set of knives and forks for me. I had dinner with her every evening, and she would serve me from her own plate. She thought that watching me eat was the funniest thing in the world.

I could have lived without seeing *her* eat, though. She was ladylike for a giant, but she still gobbled as much as twelve farmers would eat at one sitting. Her favourite dish was roasted lark, which was the size of nine Christmas turkeys. She could crunch the whole thing between her teeth, beak, bones and all.

Life would have been pleasant for me at the palace were it not for the fact that I was in danger every day because of my littleness.

I was at the mercy of another so-called little person, the mean-minded court jester. He was a midget compared with the giants, because he was only the size of a small tree. He was jealous of me.

'I was doing well before you arrived,' he hissed. 'How can I compete with those tiny little arms and legs? Bah!!'

One evening at dinner time, the jester tossed me into an enormous bowl of cream. I tried to swim in it, but it was too thick, like a swamp. I would have drowned if Glum had not fished me out in time. My new clothes were ruined, and the sour cream in my hair eventually turned to smelly cheese.

Also, he knew how much I hated flies. After all, they were as big as birds to me. I could see them landing on food and clearly leaving their poo and spawn everywhere. I could even see the slime on their feet that allowed them to walk on the ceiling. The jester would catch the flies and release them right into my face. Yuk! But I soon learned to slice them in two with my sword.

One day, I was attacked by a swarm of wasps. I killed four of them, and kept their stings as trophies; they were each at least ten centimetres long.

And as for the jester? At last, the Queen grew tired of his antics, and sent him away to the royal winter palace, where he could bother me no more.

Still, I was always in danger. All the power that I had felt in Lilliput had disappeared. I even had to ask for help every time I wanted the toilet, and I haven't done that since I was an infant!

There was one time when I nipped behind a dandelion, for a wee, without telling Glum. A dog snatched me up in his dripping fangs and carried me away to a field. He was busy burying me next to some old bones when, luckily, Glum found us.

Then there was the day I was strolling along in the garden in front of Her Majesty. I was in the mood for showing off, so I decided to leap over a fresh, steaming cow-dung on the path. Shame I had forgotten that I'm no good at the long jump. I jumped short, and landed straight into the dung, splat! right up to my neck. Everyone laughed for weeks about that one.

The worst day of all was when a pet monkey kidnapped me. It happened like this ...

I was sitting in my box with the windows wide open because it was warm. Suddenly I heard a sound. His Majesty's pet monkey had climbed in and was capering around the room!

We all know how nosey monkeys are, and it wasn't long before a hairy paw came into my box and started feeling about. I squealed and hid under my little bed, but the monkey grabbed me by the coat, dragged me out and clasped me to his hairy breast.

He might have been huge, smelly and dirty, but he was nimble. He was onto the roof in a flash, with me under his arm. Meanwhile, hundreds of metres below, Glum was screaming her head off, and the servants were rushing around, looking for a long ladder.

It was bad enough being on the roof in the arms of a monkey, but worse was yet to come. The animal insisted on feeding me. I do believe he thought I was a baby monkey! He took chewed food that he stored in his cheeks, like a hamster, and forced it down my throat with his big monkey finger. I don't know how I didn't choke. And all the while he was patting me and prodding me until I was black and blue.

Eventually the monkey was startled by all the noise and dropped me in a roof gutter. I lay there for hours, half-dead, until Glum rescued me. Later, I vomited up all the monkey's food, and had to stay in bed for two weeks.

I was homesick. The King treated me as if everything I did was a joke – including nearly being killed by a monkey the size of an elephant. I felt as if nothing I said or did was taken seriously, just because I looked so different from other people. Yet I was too little to try and escape, and anyway, Glum kept an eye on me all the time.

One day, Glum took me down to the beach in my box. She set me down on a sunny patch of sand and wandered off to look in rock pools. For the first time in weeks, I was alone.

Suddenly there was a deafening shriek, and a shadow darkened my windows. A great eagle swooped down, snatched the box with me still in it, and flew out to sea!

The last thing I saw was poor Glum crying out to me from the shore, before she disappeared behind a cloud. The eagle carried me high and far. What would my fate be when we landed? Would I:

a] Become bird food?

b] Become fish food?

c] Somehow get home in one piece?

Just as I was thinking this, I suddenly felt myself falling down, down at great speed. There was a big splash. The eagle, spying a better prey, had dropped me into the ocean.

How scared I was, as I waited to sink! My beautiful box, which I loved so much, was about to become my coffin.

But, by a miracle, a passing ship spotted me and picked me up, more dead than alive from thirst. Imagine my relief when I clapped eyes on my rescuers. They were no giants but the same size as me!

The Captain asked me many questions and I told him everything. He believed my story, honest man that he was. As proof, I showed him my treasures: the wasp stings, the gold collar that was really a ring, and my breeches made of a mouse's skin.

After many more days of sailing, I came home. I cannot describe how glad I am to be back on dry land with my family once more. Now, every night, friends gather by my fire to listen to the tales of my adventures — and they always ask for the one about Gulliver and the Land of the Giants.